A Note to Parents

For many children, learning ma[...] e math!" is their first response — to w[...] y add "Me, too!" Children often see adults comfortably reading and writing, but they rarely have such models for mathematics. And math fear can be catching!

The easy-to-read stories in this *Hello Math* series were written to give children a positive introduction to mathematics and parents a pleasurable re-acquaintance with a subject that is important to everyone's life. *Hello Math* stories make mathematical ideas accessible, interesting, and fun for children. The activities and suggestions at the end of each book provide parents with a hands-on approach to help children develop mathematical interest and confidence.

Enjoy the mathematics!

• Give your child a chance to retell the story. The more familiar children are with the story, the more they will understand its mathematical concepts.
• Use the colorful illustrations to help children "hear and see" the math at work in the story.
• Treat the math activities as games to be played for fun. Follow your child's lead. Spend time on those activities that engage your child's interest and curiosity.
• Activities, especially ones using physical materials, help make abstract mathematical ideas concrete.

Learning is a messy process and learning about math calls for children to become immersed in lively experiences that help them make sense of mathematical concepts and symbols.

Although learning about numbers is basic to math, other ideas, such as identifying shapes and patterns, measuring, collecting and interpreting data, reasoning logically, and thinking about chance are also important. By reading these stories and having fun with the activities, you will help your child enthusiastically say *"Hello, Math,"* instead of "I hate math."

—Marilyn Burns
National Mathematics Educator
Author of *The I Hate Mathematics! Book*

Library of Congress Cataloging-in-Publication Data
Stamper, Judith Bauer.
    Tic-tac-toe: three in a row/by Judith Bauer Stamper;
illustrated by Ken Wilson-Max; activities by Marilyn Burns.
        p.   cm. — (Hello math reader. Level 1)
    Summary: A boy learns how to play tic-tac-toe and improves his skills playing with a friend. Includes related activities.
    ISBN 0-590-39963-2
    [1. Tic-tac-toe — Fiction.   2. Stories in rhyme.]   I. Wilson-Max, Ken, ill.
II. Burns, Marilyn.   III. Title.   IV. Series.
PZ8.3.S78255Ti   1998
[E] — dc21   97-12852
                                                                              CIP
                                                                              AC

12   11   10   9   7   8/0

Printed in the U.S.A.   23

First printing, February 1998

Tic-Tac-Toe
Three in a Row

by Judith Bauer Stamper
Illustrated by Ken Wilson-Max
Math Activities by Marilyn Burns

Hello Math Reader — Level 1

SCHOLASTIC INC. Cartwheel ·B·O·O·K·S·®

New York Toronto London Auckland Sydney
Mexico City New Delhi Hong Kong

I'm so smart.
Now I know
how to play
tic-tac-toe!

Make an X,
then an O.

Three across.
Tic-tac-toe!

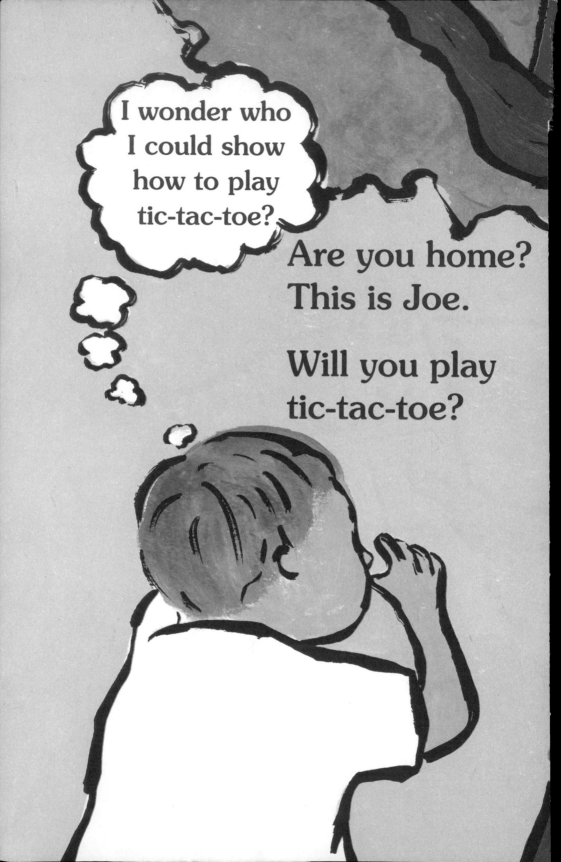

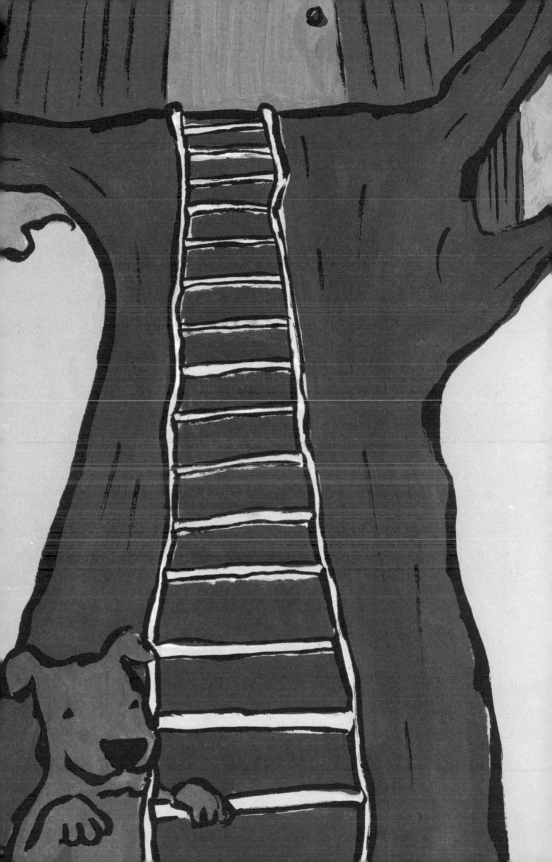

Who is there?
Well, hello.

I like to play
tic-tac-toe.

You go first.
Don't be slow.

I play fast.
Tic-tac-toe.

X, X, X. That's a row—
up and down. Tic-tac-toe.

Try again. Now you go.
Think about tic-tac-toe.

Three more X's.
No, no, no!

You won again.
Tic-tac-toe.

If you want,
I could show
you the rules.
Tic-tac-toe.

Start on top,
or below.
Take your time.
Tic-tac-toe.

Three across—
that's a row.

X, X, X.
Tic-tac-toe.

Up and down,
O, O, O,

also works.
Tic-tac-toe.

Here's another
way to go—

side to side.
Tic-tac-toe.

Thanks a lot!
Now I know
how to play
tic-tac-toe.

Make an X,
then an O.

Will you play
tic-tac-toe?

• ABOUT THE ACTIVITIES •

Tic-tac-toe is a game that fascinates and delights young children. They enjoy figuring out how to draw the tic-tac-toe game board and easily learn how to take turns placing X's or O's. The game also has the benefit of giving children the opportunity to reason logically, an important aspect of mathematical thinking. (As a matter of fact, studying game strategies intrigues many mathematicians and is included in university mathematics courses.)

While learning to play tic-tac-toe isn't difficult for many young children, learning what to do to win or to avoid losing isn't obvious. They need a good deal of time and experience playing the game to figure out how to play strategically.

This book can be enjoyed by children who haven't yet learned about tic-tac-toe as well as by those who already can play the game. The story models the game and shows children different ways to place X's or O's in order to win.

After reading the story with your child, try playing tic-tac-toe together. Then try some of the activities included here. Be open to your child's interests and enjoy the math!

— Marilyn Burns

Retelling the Story

Reread the story and look for the tic-tac-toe games as you go.

In the first game, Joe shows his dog how he can win. He made three X's across the top. Point to the winning row of X's.

When Joe plays with the girl, she wins with three X's down the middle. Point to her winning row of X's.

The girl wins again with three X's on a slant. Point to her winning X's.

Then the girl helps Joe win. He makes three X's across the middle. Point to Joe's winning row of X's.

The girl shows Joe how to win by going up and down. Point to the row of O's from top to bottom.

The girl shows Joe another way three O's can go on a slant. Point to the row of O's on a slant.

New vocabulary is best learned in the context of an activity. Use the X's and O's to help your child learn the vocabulary for positions—up, down, left, right, across, on a slant, and so on.

Winning Rows of O's

Here are the eight different ways to win tic-tac-toe with a row of O's. (You could also win the same ways if you put X's where the O's are.)

Half of the ways have an O in the space that is in the middle of the tic-tac-toe board. Find these four boards.

Fancy Words

Here are three words that tell how the O's or X's go — horizontal, vertical, and diagonal. They may be hard to read, but they aren't hard to understand. Use the tic-tac-toe boards on page 30 to help you scc what these words mean.

When O's (or X's) go across, they are horizontal. Point to the three tic-tac-toe boards with O's that are horizontal.

When O's (or X's) go straight up and down, they are vertical. Point to the three tic-tac-toe boards with O's that are vertical.

When O's (or X's) go on a slant, they are diagonal. Point to the two tic-tac-toe boards with O's that are diagonal.

If your child is interested in practicing these three words, look through the story and use horizontal, vertical, and diagonal to describe the pictures whenever possible.

Four-in-a-Row

To win at tic-tac-toe, you have to get three X's or O's in a row.

To play four-in-a-row, you need a larger game board. And to win at four-in-a-row, you have to get four X's or O's in a row. Try playing this game and see what happens.

More Four-in-a-Row Games

Try playing four-in-a-row with a larger board, like one of these two.

Do you think these games are harder to win or easier?

Now try playing a game on one of the larger boards with three people. One of you is X, one of you is O, and one of you is A.